No one knows for sure how Pooh got his name. But whenever a fly settled on his nose he said "Pooh!" to blow it away – so perhaps that's why he came to be called Winnie the Pooh.

Winnie the Pooh liked to have 'A Little Something' around eleven o'clock every morning. Best of all he liked honey. So one day Pooh went out to find the honey tree... and had a dreadful time with some very angry bees...

British Library Cataloguing in Publication Data
Walt Disney's Winnie the Pooh and the honey tree.
I. Disney, Walt, *1901-1966*
813'.54 [J]
ISBN 0-7214-1196-7

First edition

Published by Ladybird Books Ltd Loughborough Leicestershire UK

Printed in England

Disney

WINNIE THE POOH
and the Honey Tree

Ladybird Books

Winnie the Pooh was very fond of honey. He could lick out a honey pot until there was nothing left except a little bit of stickiness round the rim.

Every morning at about eleven o'clock Pooh liked to have A Little Something. And that Little Something was usually honey.

Pooh was so greedy that he could eat a whole pot of honey and still feel hungry.

He ate and ate and his tummy got

fatter and fatter. Then one day he
burst at the seams, and his friend
Christopher Robin had to mend
him with a needle and thread.

Pooh decided it was time to do his
stoutness exercises. As he did them,
he hummed a tune so that the
exercises wouldn't seem such hard
work.

He stretched his short arms up in the air, then bent down to touch his toes. He did try very hard, but he couldn't quite reach them.

Pooh had just sat down to have a rest when he suddenly heard a buzzing sound. And he knew what made that buzzing sound – bees.

Bees meant only one thing to Pooh – honey.

He was sitting under a honey tree!

At once Pooh started to climb the honey tree. As he climbed, he hummed a little tune to himself.

He was so busy climbing and humming that he didn't notice how thin the branches were.

All of a sudden there was a loud CRACK! The branch Pooh was holding snapped, and he slipped. Then he bounced from branch to branch, and landed with a crash in a gorse bush.

Poor old Pooh! He crawled out of
the bush and picked the prickles
out of his fur. He was now a very
cross, hungry little bear.

Then Pooh had an idea. He went
to see his friend Christopher
Robin.

"I wonder," said Pooh, "if you've
such a thing as a balloon about
you?"

"Why do you want a balloon?"
asked Christopher Robin.

Pooh put his paw to his mouth and
said in a deep whisper, "Honey!"

"No one gets honey with balloons!" said Christopher Robin.

"I do," replied Pooh. "When you go after honey, you mustn't let the bees know you're coming. So if I have a blue balloon, they may think I'm only part of the sky."

He thought for a moment, then he added, "I shall try to look like a small black cloud. That will trick them." And he rolled about in a muddy puddle until he was black all over.

Christopher Robin thought Pooh was being rather silly, but since he did have a blue balloon, he gave it to Pooh.

Pooh took the balloon, and almost at once a gust of wind lifted him up into the air.

He floated up towards the honey
tree, then stretched out his paw and
scooped up some delicious honey.

He was feeling very pleased with
himself, until he saw that his paw
was covered with bees. They were
buzzing angrily.

"Oh dear!" cried Pooh. "I think
the bees suspect something!" Then
he shouted to Christopher Robin
who was down below, "I say,
Christopher Robin, you could help
me to trick the bees! Put up

your umbrella and say, 'Oh my, it
looks like rain!'"

Christopher Robin put up his
umbrella. "Oh my, it looks like
rain!" he said.

But the bees continued to buzz angrily around Pooh.

Then the string holding Pooh's balloon came undone and the air inside escaped with a rush.

Pooh went zooming through the sky
at great speed, then landed safely in
Christopher Robin's arms.

But the bees went on buzzing, "Thief!
Thief! You tried to steal our honey!"

Then Christopher Robin had an idea. He and Pooh jumped into the muddy puddle and hid under the umbrella. The bees would not find them there.

Pooh was pleased to be sitting in a muddy puddle. It was one of his most favourite places to play.

The bees buzzed around angrily for a while, looking for Pooh and Christopher Robin, but they couldn't see them. The umbrella made a good hiding place.

At last the bees returned to their
tree, and Christopher Robin and
Pooh crept out from their hiding
place. They looked just like *two*
little black rainclouds now!

By the time they were clean again, Pooh decided he could do with A Little Something.

He picked up one of his honey pots, and ate and ate until his tummy was full.

He was a very happy, very sticky little bear. He had had a terrible adventure with the bees, but the day had ended splendidly after all.